What happens when a young girl with a Hall of Fame baseball pedigree breaks the family mold and follows her dream to become a soul singer? *Roxy Rogers: Your Destiny Is Calling* helps children see that their families will love them just the same when they pursue their true passions in life.

Library of Congress Control Number: 2014944689
ISBN: 978-0-692-24871-3

Printed in the United States of America

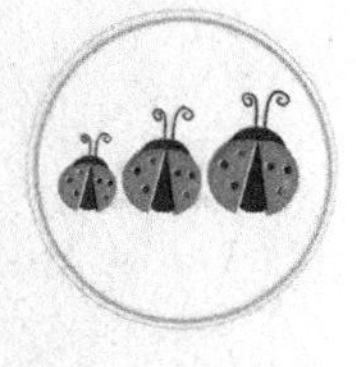

Three-Bug Books
www.threebugbooks.com

Written by Emily Siskin-Toy
Illustrated by Brian C. Krümm

Emily Siskin-Toy and Three-Bug Books are excited to launch *Roxy Rogers: Your Destiny Is Calling*. Roxy bears a close resemblance to Emily's real-life daughter, whose youth softball and basketball teams Emily coached for several years. It turns out she had a different desire, much to her mom's surprise!

Brian C. Krümm follows the flow of fate as best he can, bouncing from basketball to snowboarding to music to art. Currently based in the San Francisco Bay Area, he has illustrated numerous picture books, including the award-winning *My First Sikh Books*. Visit him online at www.brianartwork.com.

Written By: Emily Siskin-Toy

Illustrated By: Brian C. Krümm

For Tommy and Maddy, the two bugs that make my life complete —E.S.T.

For Dad, Mom, and Christy —B.K.

Roxy Rogers yanked the covers over her head, as the dreaded day was just hours away.

It was nearly time to do what everybody said she was born to do.

Not long after she wobbled her first steps and babbled her first word (it was "ball"), Roxy's family began training her to become...

"It's etched in stone," her family cheered when she whacked the ball into their neighbor's yard when she was just four.

Roxy searched and searched for that stone. She wanted to throw it to the bottom of the ocean.

"It's your destiny!" Great-Grandpa Abe announced. He played for the New York Yankees with the amazing Joe DiMaggio in 1937.

"It's in your genes," Great-Grandma Roxy reminded her namesake. During World War II, she was a star pitcher for the Rockford Peaches of the All-American Girls Professional Baseball League.

"You're as strong as an ox," remarked Grandpa Leo. He hit home runs by the bushel for the 1950s Brooklyn Dodgers alongside the inspiring Jackie Robinson.

"You've got a cannon for an arm," her dad said when they played catch. In the 1980s, he was a star right fielder for the Los Angeles Dodgers.

“You’re tall for your age,” her big sister, Morgan, pointed out when Roxy snared pop flies with ease. Morgan won a gold medal playing center field for Team USA in the 2000 Olympics in Sydney, Australia.

"You really like to get dirty when you play ball," her mom said proudly when she did the laundry.

Her college team nicknamed her "the vacuum cleaner"...

...because she sucked up every ground ball that dared come her way.

But none of this mattered much to Roxy. She liked softball, but she loved something else.

When her family wasn't paying attention, Roxy snuck out her mom's old soul music records, and sang into her homemade microphone.

She didn't daydream of hitting softballs to the moon. She always imagined herself dressed up on stage belting out the music of her favorite songstress, Aretha Franklin, the Queen of Soul.

Roxy marched with her team in the big softball parade through town.
She sang Aretha Franklin songs to pass the time.
She couldn't wait for the day to be over.

But then something happened,
and it changed Roxy's life forever.

When the parade gathered in the center of town the mayor had an announcement. It seemed that the lady whose job it was to sing "The Star-Spangled Banner" was stuck in traffic.

"I think I heard one of our softball players singing earlier today," said the mayor. "Could that little girl please come to the stage and help us out?"

Roxy couldn't believe her ears, and to the shock of her family, she raced up to the stage and took the microphone.

"Roxy sings?"
asked a shocked Grandpa Leo.

"I don't think so,"
Roxy's father said.

"It couldn't be,"
echoed Roxy's mother.

Roxy stared straight at her family and...

SANG with everything that she was
and everything that she wanted to be.

She shimmied and grooved and amazed just like her soul sister, Aretha.

Roxy bowed to the grand cheers and applause; her skin tingled, her heart raced.

"That's who I am," said Roxy to her family. "*That* is my destiny."

And from that day forward, Roxy's singing bounced sweetly around the house...

...much to the delight of her biggest fans.

Did you find all of the hidden clues that Roxy's true love is music? Go back and count them. You can find 48 total, beginning with the treble clef on page two. Have fun!

Historical Figures:

Who was Joe DiMaggio?

Nicknamed "The Yankee Clipper," Joe DiMaggio is widely considered one of the greatest baseball players of all time. He played for the Yankees from 1936 - 1951, winning three Most-Valuable-Player awards and hitting in a record 56 straight games in the 1941 season. DiMaggio was elected into the National Baseball Hall of Fame in 1955.

Who was Jackie Robinson?

Jackie Robinson broke baseball's color barrier when he joined the Brooklyn Dodgers in 1947. Known for his exceptional speed on the basepaths, Robinson stole 197 bases overall in his 10 years with the Dodgers, including an incredible 19 swipes of home. Robinson was named National League Most-Valuable-Player in 1949, and was elected into the National Baseball Hall of Fame in 1962.

Who is Aretha Franklin?

Born in Memphis, Tennessee, on March 25, 1942, Aretha Franklin earned her nickname, "The Queen of Soul," for her amazing vocal talents and immense popularity. At a very young age, Franklin sang in her reverend father's church, and she recorded her first gospel song at 14. She had 10 Top 10 radio hits between early 1967 and late 1968 for Atlantic Records, including "Chain of Fools," "Think," and "Respect."

What was the All-American Girls Professional Baseball League (AAGPBL)?

During World War II, chewing gum mogul Phillip K. Wrigley, who also owned the Chicago Cubs, feared that his and other teams' major league players would be drafted into the war, perhaps leading to the collapse of Major League Baseball. To prepare for this possibility, he helped form a professional league that consisted of America's best women softball players. The AAGPBL launched with four teams in 1943 to large, enthusiastic crowds. Wrigley's fears never came true as the war ended in 1945, but the women's league lived on until 1954.

CPSIA information can be obtained at www.ICGtesting.com
Printed in the USA
BVOW10*1705240914

368060BV00002BA/4/P

9 780692 248713